Map
of
Julie's
Journey

MARKET STREET

GOOSEBERRY AVENUE

CLOVER
HILL

MOSS
PLACE

PRIMROSE

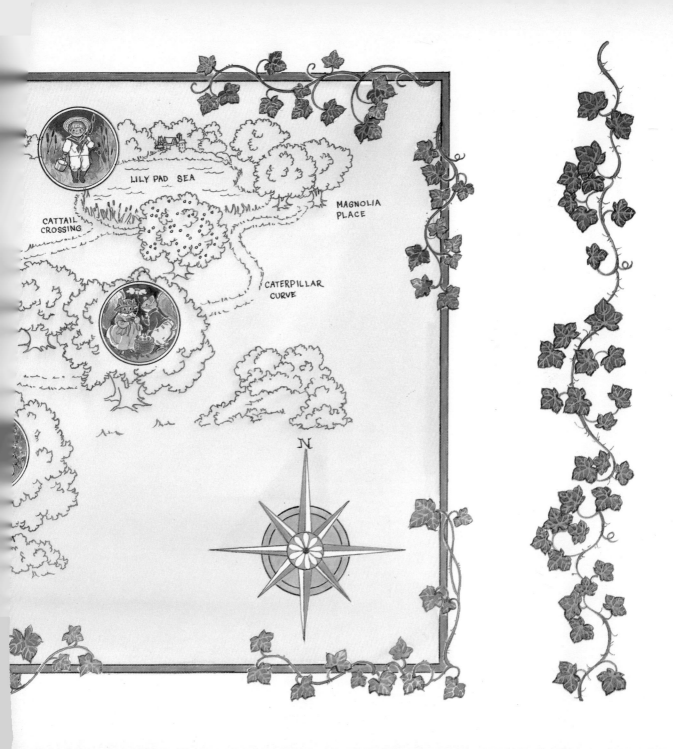

LILY PAD SEA

CATTAIL
CROSSING

MAGNOLIA
PLACE

CATERPILLAR
CURVE

N

® Landoll, Inc.
Ashland, Ohio 44805
Copyright © 1995 by The American Design Company
Artwork Copyright © 1995 by the American Design Company
All Rights Reserved.
For information pertaining to "Julie's Journey" contact:
**SHERRY M. JOHNSON, DIRECTOR**
**THE AMERICAN DESIGN COMPANY**
**PO BOX 15144**
**HATTIESBURG, MS 39402**

Julie's Journey

Klaus' Voyage
to Hollyander

Julie Wyatt Schenk

Illustrated by Mildred Wyatt

"What shall we do today, Julie?" asked Edward, as they strolled casually along the path just past the garden gate.

"Well," said Julie, giving the question some thought. "Mother has made some brownies – we could have a picnic down by the pond."

"Splendid!" pronounced Edward, stooping by an oak tree and picking a blade of grass to hold between his teeth. "Hey, look at this!" he said suddenly.

Julie stooped to examine Edward's findings. "What is it?" she inquired.

"This tulip. It looks just like the ones at our house. Dad ordered them specially from Holland. They're supposed to be rare, so he planted them around a little windmill in the back of the house." A smile crossed Edward's face. "Wouldn't he have a regular fit if he knew we found one here in the forest?" he said, picturing his father's face. "And isn't it funny that it's growing here, in front of Klaus' tree?"

Julie stared at the oak tree in front of her. This was it, all right; there was no doubting it. This was *his* tree, Klaus' tree, with its huge, fern-covered roots surrounded by neat clumps of primroses, Forget-Me-Nots and hollyhocks. And that tulip. That tulip. Julie, well aware of Klaus' passion for beautiful flowers, knew that he wouldn't have been able to resist such a fine specimen, once he knew it existed. But how did he know about it? She pictured the little mouse secretly digging the hole and dropping the tulip bulb into its depths. And how did he get it *here*? For Julie could only guess at the events which had taken place, which I shall tell you about now.

laus F. Maus was a gardener; there was no doubt about that. His family had learned the art in the Old Country, with its windmills and brightly-colored tulips many generations ago. Great Grandpapa had brought the talent with him when he came to the New Land on a fine sailing ship. (Klaus had often heard the story of Great Grandpapa's perils on the open sea, of the storms and the huge waves which had nearly sunk the ship.)

Klaus' gardening heritage could be seen everywhere one looked; his clumps of primroses (the largest anyone could imagine) almost glowed as the morning sun beamed upon their pert, little faces. His Forget-Me-Nots seemed to dance as they shook off the blanket of dew which had covered them in the night. And the delphiniums and foxgloves – they stood like soldiers at attention, dressed in their most stately uniforms. Gentians, nasturtiums, Bells of Ireland – Klaus took care of them all, watering them regularly, pruning them when necessary.

Klaus leaned on his rake, admiring the particular beauty of the flowers on so quiet a morning. He had worked hard, and it showed. The silence was soon broken, however, by the sound of soft footsteps on the narrow path leading from the deeper woods. Klaus glanced at the sun. Yes, it was about time, he surmised. "Hello, Katrina," he said, as the ruffle of her white petticoat came into view.

"Hello, Klaus," said a neatly dressed little brown mouse, as she picked her way through the Forget-Me-Nots. She carried a little silver tray, covered with a checkered napkin. "I've brought you something," she said, smiling sweetly. Such actions would have been, in company other than Klaus', unthinkable for Katrina. She was, in fact, an extremely timid little mouse. She considered herself plain and homely in looks (which was not true); she never entertained, for she thought no one would want to visit her (which was also not true). She spent most of her time at home, sewing, making laces and baking.

But with Klaus, it was different. He never acted as though her plainness bothered him, and he never seemed to expect her to make witty remarks or intellectual statements. In fact, he seemed to expect nothing from her at all, except for her admiration of his garden. And that's how it was on this day.

"Look here, Katrina," he said, taking a delicately decorated cookie from her tray and waving his arm across the garden. "They're beautiful today, aren't they?"

"Why, yes, Klaus, they are; I've never seen anything so pretty," she said truthfully, for she admired anything that was able to be beautiful.

"And over here," Klaus said, as they wandered through the garden to the far corner, "is where I've put some new seeds. The girl, Julie, left them for me. I found them the other day, in the mailbox."

Katrina nodded and smiled. "Yes, Julie is kind; she does things like that for all the forest animals. Why, just yesterday she brought me a beautiful piece of floral chintz. I'll make it into some lovely cushions with ruffles around the edges...."

"M-m-m...they'll be hollyhocks, I think," Klaus said proudly, still pointing at the patch of dirt.  He hadn't heard a word she said.

"Oh, they'll be perfect there," Katrina said, smiling.  "In fact, the whole garden will be perfect."

"No," sighed Klaus, shaking his head and pointing to a bare spot in the corner of the garden.  "Not perfect.  I still have one spot reserved for a very special flower.  When I find it, *then* it will be perfect."

And so it went, once or twice a week. Katrina visited, bringing with her baked goods of every variety, including little flower-shaped cookies which she made especially for Klaus; they were her way of expressing her gratitude for his company. She shared the contents of her tray with Klaus, who then gave her a royal tour of the garden, pointing out new additions and changes along the way. "This is new," he would say about a grouping of Dutchman's Breeches. "You don't see blooms like *that* very often." And Katrina would agree, for her passion for beautiful flowers was as great as Klaus'.

Klaus did not spend *all* his time in the garden, however. He also enjoyed fishing excursions to the pond. "The Great Lilypad Sea," he called it, for it seemed as big to him as an ocean does to you and me. In fact, he believed it to be the very ocean Grandpapa had crossed all those years ago.

Klaus had fashioned a fishing pole from a discarded toothpick and some sewing thread. As he sat on the edge of the pond one day, waiting for the minnows to bite, he watched the cool water lap at his toes. At once, something hard struck his foot. He picked the object up carefully.

It was a glass disc, about the diameter of two primroses (for Klaus measured everything by flowers). It had a carved wooden handle and was ringed in shiny gold metal. Carefully, he stood the disc on its edge and looked through it. A monstrous winged creature stared back at him; Klaus squeaked with terror and turned to run, letting the glass fall. He looked back; the monster was gone. In its place hovered a harmless blue butterfly. Klaus picked up the glass again. The monster returned. 'A spyglass!' he thought to himself. Great Grandpapa had told stories about pirates' spyglasses, and about how they used them to see lands far off. "I wonder..." said Klaus aloud.

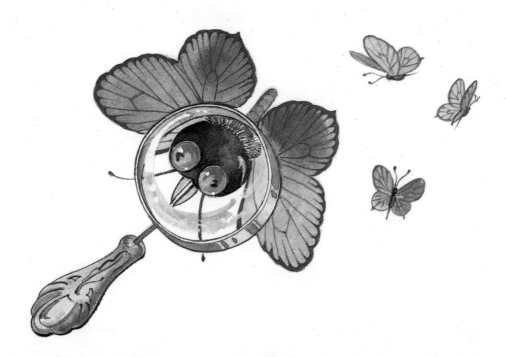

He raised the glass in the direction of the water and looked through it. "Land!" he squeaked. "It's the other side of the ocean!" He looked again. He saw fluffy, green bushes and – what was that? A windmill – it must be Hollyander! (Because Klaus' interest lay mostly in flowers, he had never studied much about geography, or about the proper names of countries.)

Klaus savored his new discovery in his mind. Hollyander! That's where his special flower would grow. Now, if he could only manage to get there! He scurried home, forgetting about his minnows. He must have a sailboat!

or two days, he gathered the items he would need for his boat. A dried magnolia leaf with curled edges would serve nicely as the boat itself.

Katrina visited him as he worked feverishly. "I've made you something special," she said shyly. "It's a seedcake – a special recipe of my grandmother's. I looked for it all week long."

Klaus grunted. "Really, Katrina," he said, polishing his leaf vigorously. "I've no time for your silly prattle about seeds and cakes. "I've got *important* work to do."

"I'm sorry, Klaus," Katrina said, her voice trembling. "I won't bother you anymore." And she left.

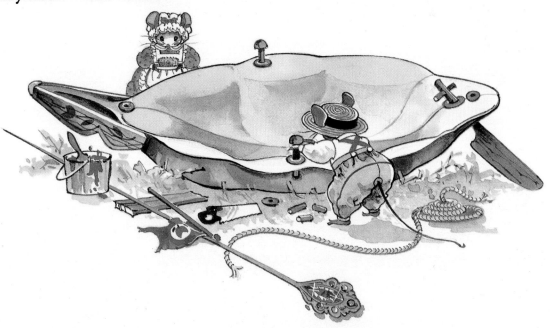

For the mast of his boat, Klaus chose a large hatpin. But the sail – what about the sail? Wait; what had Katrina said the other day? Julie had brought her some chintz. Yes, some chintz!

Early the next morning, Klaus dressed and stole quietly over to Katrina's cottage beneath the large hydrangea bush at Moss Place. He had never been there before, and he marveled at the size of the blooms on the bush. They were the largest he had ever seen, and their color was the most delicate shade of blue. The house and surrounding area were neat and clean, with white lace curtains in the windows and little colored glass beads which formed the walkway to the front door. He went around back. A wooden arched swing sat nestled underneath a honeysuckle vine. No doubt Julie had gotten it for her. The whole place was quite pretty, really.

But Klaus forgot about looking around when he spied the object of his visit. In a corner of the mossy backyard, he saw a clothesline, on which a freshly washed piece of floral chintz fluttered in the breeze. "No use waking Katrina," Klaus reasoned. "She wouldn't mind if I took it. Besides, I'll bring it back when I'm done with it, or I'll get her another piece; but I haven't got time to worry about that *now*." And he scurried back home, dragging the chintz behind him.

The sailboat was ready. Klaus packed his provisions — some nuts and edible seeds, mostly, along with a few berries and his favorite hat — and started on his way. It was fine day for sailing; clouds billowed across the blue sky and a silent breeze pushed the little boat along toward the other side of the water. Klaus ate a few seeds and dozed periodically, keeping himself on course with his spyglass and a trusty compass given to him by Great Grandpapa. The whole trip took a day and a half. When at last a gentle breeze nudged the boat against the far shore, Klaus wasted no time. He secured the boat to a sturdy cattail and scurried up the hill to the windmill.

ven as he recalled the stories about the Old Country which had been passed down to him from his great grandfather, Klaus was not at all prepared for what he saw. What seemed to him an ocean of tulip plants, some of them blooming, swept up to meet his nearsighted little eyes. He rolled. He squeaked. He waltzed among the graceful stems of the tulips, giddy with pleasure. Which one – which one, of all these perfect specimens, should he choose? At last, he settled upon a large bulb, next to the windmill, which he felt certain would contain a spectacular flower.

He dug to the base of the bulb, expertly shaking the dirt from the fleshy roots at the center. He rolled the bulb in a scrap of moist burlap from his napsack; this would keep the roots moist and protected from the sun on the journey back. Carefully, he rolled the bulb down the hill and hoisted it onto the boat. Flushed with excitement and a sense of great accomplishment, Klaus began his long journey home.

It was mid-afternoon of the same day of his arrival and the breeze which had brought him gently to the shore had turned into a not-so-gentle wind. "All the better," said Klaus, as he patted his prize bulb. "We'll get home sooner." In his excitement, he had forgotten Great-Grandpapa's first rule of sea safety: "If you must travel by sea," he had warned, "first consult the skies." Klaus was midway into his journey by the time he remembered this rule. It was too late. The dark clouds which had hovered in the sky crashed together, pouring forth huge torrents of water, and the wind had become an angry gale. Klaus could do nothing but ride the storm out, bailing out his leaf as the water spilled in. At last, the storm subsided; the little boat floated feebly to its home shore, its chintz sail tattered by the buffeting winds. Klaus, exhausted, dragged his precious bulb up the bank, up the hill, and to his home, where he planted it the next morning.

The tulip grew larger each day until at last the morning dawned which brought the opening of the large, pink bud. Klaus trembled all over with excitement as he watched the tulip glisten in the dew. Yes, he thought joyously, Katrina will certainly love this! And he waited for the sound of her footsteps. But Katrina didn't come that day. Or the next. Or the next. Klaus paced back and forth in his garden. Where was she? She must see this, or else... Or else it wouldn't be the same, he realized. It wasn't necessarily the flowers in his garden that had brought him such joy – it was his pleasure in sharing them with Katrina.

laus made his decision quickly. He snipped off the tulip at its base and carried it to Katrina's house. There was no answer at the front door; he walked around back. He found Katrina sitting in her swing, sewing. She looked up and smiled shyly as he approached her. "It bloomed," Klaus said simply, as he held the tulip up for her to see.

"I see," she said, still smiling.

"It's for you. I'm sorry, Katrina," he said gently, handing the tulip to her. For Klaus truly realized the meaning of friendship, and his heart had never beat as happily as it did when he gave away his most prized possession to his *best* friend, Katrina.